THE
EMERALD
SWORD

BRANDON HOLLIS

The Emerald Sword

Copyright © 2024 by Brandon Hollis.

This publication contains the opinions and ideas of its author. It is intended to provide helpful and informative material on the subjects addressed in the publication. The author and publisher specifically disclaim all responsibility for any liability, loss, or risk, personal or otherwise, which is incurred as a consequence, directly or indirectly, of the use and application of any of the contents of this book.

MILTON & HUGO L.L.C.
4407 Park Ave., Suite 5
Union City, NJ 07087, USA

Website: www. miltonandhugo.com
Hotline: 1- 888-778-0033
Email: info@miltonandhugo.com

Ordering Information:
Quantity sales. Special discounts are available on quantity purchases by corporations, associations, and others. For details, contact the publisher at the address above.

Library of Congress Control Number: 2024907812
ISBN-13:   979-8-89285-056-8   [Paperback Edition]
               979-8-89285-057-5   [Hardback Edition]
               979-8-89285-055-1   [Digital Edition]

Rev. date: 03/28/2024

THE
EMERALD
SWORD

BRANDON HOLLIS

PROLOGUE

THE CREATION
OF THE WORLD

 here is one, the Unknown Being, who alone is lord and creator of the world and its inhabitants. In the blink of an eye, in an instant, all came to be as it is. He willed it, and the oceans roared, the rivers churned, the mountains rose, the winds blew, and plants and animals were brought forth from the earth. But then the Unknown Being decided to create other beings somewhat similar to himself, yet still inferior. They were to be immortal, quite fair looking, and very wise. These are known as the First Created, the Immortals. Only two were created, however: Endiril and Gwentythe. Gwentythe had been given the gift of foresight and was and is still known as the Great Priestess. These two procreated, and the three priestesses came into existence; and even though the offspring of Immortals, the priestesses themselves were not immortal. You see, Immortals cannot die even in battle against lesser beings, but the three priestesses were mortal not because

of the powers they possessed (fire, earth and water), but because of the greed and selfish ambition for greater power that haunted them. An Immortal can defeat or even kill another Immortal in battle only if another power is wielded from outside the Immortal, either through magic or an enchanted weapon or piece of armor, or one of the same from heaven itself, forged by the Unknown. In a great battle for immortal supremacy, the priestesses destroyed themselves. Gwentythe, the Great Priestess, is the only priestess left.

After this had transpired, the Unknown then created mortals, the Second Created, with the sole purpose to worship and serve the Immortals and their offspring (should Endiril and Gwentythe procreate again), for the Unknown had decreed that only Immortals may worship him and does not allow the Second Created to do so. Soon after this, the Unknown commanded Endiril to rule all the land and the Second Created and to bring forth *one* heir to rule after Endiril had left the land. The Unknown had decreed that Endiril may live in the land five hundred years, then must leave to an island paradise specially made for Immortal males by the Unknown. The island is known as Allahalav, island eternal. Gwentythe, being female and unable to inherit, shall dwell with mortals for the rest of time as commanded by the Unknown. She dwells to this day in a great temple called the Temple of the Priestesses, and that is where the mortals worship her. This temple is located in Endiril's fortress.

Sometime after the Second Created were created, Endiril and Gwentythe procreated, and Andiril came forth. But they went against the Unknown's command and brought forth a second heir, Gūrond. Almost immediately after Gūrond's birth, Gwentythe used her foresight to predict a great feud between Andiril and Gūrond. Because of this transgression, the Unknown punished the Immortals in having Andiril and Gūrond at odds with each other. Until of course one of them is destroyed.

Endiril took no heed of his wife's foresight and at the age of 400 left for Allahalav—100 years early. By this time, Andiril was 203 years old and Gūrond 202 years old. Before leaving, Endiril had been deceived by Gūrond. Gūrond accepted only the eastern third of Endiril's kingdom, as well as acting as if he would stay on good terms with Andiril. Even though Gūrond accepted only a third of the kingdom, the Eastern part was greater in population, wealth, and number of cities and towns than its Western counterpart. The choice to leave early was a costly one, for shortly after Endiril had left, Gūrond started building fortifications along his border with the West, as well as massing an enormous army from the mortals within his lands.

LATER HISTORY

he kingdom is divided. The frontier garrisons of Andiril have for two decades been at war, the Great War, with the frontier garrisons of Gūrond. However, good and evil in this conflict can only be distinguished by motive. Ever has Gūrond, Ruler of the East, been planning to wage war with his brother Andiril, Ruler of the West. Ever has Gūrond wished to rule all the land as their father had done. He has wished to exploit its wealth and enslave every soul living in his domain. Even before the days of peace, before Gūrond first started attacking Andiril, has he been planning this war-torn age.

'Twas not always so. Because Andiril was the firstborn, Gūrond was jealous. Gūrond thought of himself as a more able ruler and on top of this was a renowned hunter. To hunt, javelins were used, which require great skill to master. It has to be thrown accurately, as well as hard enough to penetrate deep enough into the flesh to kill the prey. Because of Gūrond's arrogance, the Great War was just about inevitable.

When Andiril and Gūrond first came of age to inherit their parts of the kingdom, Endiril had a pair of steel gauntlets enchanted by Gwentythe. Endiril then gave one gauntlet to each of his sons, to signify the peace that was supposed to have followed. Gūrond wears his on his left hand; but as Andiril was locking his deep in his fortress, an agent of Gūrond, no doubt, stole Andiril's gauntlet. However, the Unknown had different plans. He is master of all, so he caused Gūrond's agent to hide the gauntlet in a tower on top of the mountains near Andiril's fortress instead of bringing it directly to Gūrond. When Gūrond's agent came back empty-handed, Gūrond had him killed in a fit of rage without first asking where the gauntlet was hidden. Since then, Gūrond has been looking in vain for the gauntlet. If Gūrond should find it, the magic used to enchant the gauntlets will be unleashed, and Gūrond will be able to overwhelm Andiril. You see, two Immortals who fight each other would not be able to defeat the other in his own strength. Magic would be the decisive factor, whether in an enchanted item or aide from the Priestess or the Unknown Being.

It is important to note that warfare was unheard of before the Great War. Because of this, certain weapons have not been invented yet or are newcomers. Siege equipment is one of these newcomers. Before Gūrond, no one had heard of siege towers or catapults. Even the sword came into play shortly after Gūrond inherited the East. Javelins and spears were the only weapons before Gūrond and Andiril, and these were always used for hunting, never for maiming another soul. However, another weapon, a long-range projectile, has yet to come around; can you guess what that might be?

CHAPTER 1

 ur epic tale starts in the midst of the Great War. It has been going on for twenty years. Gwentythe has predicted that within one year, the Great War will end in a massive battle between Gūrond and Andiril, and one of her sons will be taken up by the Unknown Being and told the secret of how to win the war. The other will be taken down to the mortal Netherworld. Gūrond will be taken to one of these two places first and Andiril to the other place after. Neither Andiril nor anyone else will know to which place Gūrond will be taken, nor will Gūrond know where he will be taken until that time comes.

In the mortal Netherworld, the one taken there will be given a riddle. In the riddle will be a clue of how to successfully defend against the other taken to the Unknown. After this vision first appeared to Gwentythe, she summoned both of her sons to the Great Temple that they may hear her prophecy. This is important because no one knows how a fight between two Immortals can be drawn to a conclusion (the second offspring of the two Immortals are considered Immortals as well).

"So one of us will know the secret of defeating an Immortal and the other how to defend against the secret?" asked Gūrond.

"Yes," replied Gwentythe. "However, no one but the Unknown Being knows what the secret is or to whom he will tell it. For now, only your armies will carry out the war until your questions are answered. Until then, you two are not to physically fight each other. And you, Gūrond, may even find the other gauntlet when all is said and done."

"But why waste all those lives of the mortals? What could be the purpose of that?" asked Andiril with an aggressive tone in his voice.

"Your compassion for the mortals is not necessary. They are below us. We are greater than they. The only place they have in this world is to serve and worship us, the Immortals," answered Gwentythe. "The Unknown has a set plan for all that transpires. Everything comes into place by his guidance."

"See, brother? I told you that was their only purpose," said Gūrond.

"Servanthood is one thing. Forced slavery is another!" shouted Andiril.

"Enough! This bickering is pointless. Go, you two, out of my sight," demanded Gwentythe.

The two brothers then went their separate ways after humbly bowing to their mother. Upon the return of Andiril to his throne room, the commander of the frontier garrison, Hamai, reported to Andiril. Hamai was a great hunter, the greatest among mortals. He was the hero of the West. Hamai's skills with the sword and javelin were second in the entire world only to Gūrond and Andiril (both being Immortals, their skills were equal, thus showing how arrogant Gūrond was as he thought his skills were above Andiril's). This being said, Hamai was the most obvious choice to lead Andiril's army. After bowing and asking permission to speak, Hamai updated the Ruler of the West (as Andiril was called) on what was happening on the border.

"The Ruler of the East is starting to advance the entire Imperial Army towards the frontier of your lands, my lord," reported Hamai.

"Triple the number of men on the frontier and send word to every village that half of all the men are needed to defend the kingdom of the West," ordered Andiril. "They are to report here at the fortress."

"Yes, sir. Right away." After bowing one last time, Hamai was off.

Aside from smallish skirmishes, Gūrond had tried invading the West twice before, failing both times to conquer it. The first time was an utter disaster. Gūrond had lost every last soul he ordered to invade. The second time, Gūrond's forces advanced all the way to Andiril's fortress before having to withdraw from taking an alarming number of casualties during the siege. But this time, Gūrond was bent on complete victory. The size of his new Imperial Army was proof of this: 675,000 men, 200 catapults, and 60 siege towers. Before being summoned by his mother to the temple, Gūrond had ordered his army to slowly advance so as not to arrive at the border too quickly. Just as soon as Gūrond was arriving back at his gargantuan fortress, his army was being spotted by Hamai, the commander of Andiril's forces.

Gūrond had given his commanders very strict orders: conquer every village, slay all the women and children, and force every able-bodied man into the Imperial Army. Those unable to fight would be slain. He also ordered his army to march in front of the siege equipment so as not to lose any needed military machines for the siege of Andiril's fortress.

Gūrond's army continued to advance, seen only by their torches as it was past nightfall and hellishly dark. The frontier garrison of the West prepared for the inevitable battle ahead. Hamai said a few words of encouragement, but these had little effect. Every one of the maybe forty-five thousand border guards knew that Gūrond's army was vastly larger. When the Imperial Army was within one hundred yards, the order was given to charge. Soon, first blood was spilled. As the Imperial Army rushed to meet the Western garrison, javelins were thrown. Each side exchanged a volley of javelins, then the Imperial Army charged to the front line of the West. Hamai was waiting for the Easterners at the front as he was courageous and never demanded of others what he was not willing to do himself. As soon as the enemy was close enough, Hamai unleashed his fury unto the invaders. With every swing of his sword, he brought down an Easterner. Many times bringing down multiple Easterners. His valor was seen by others, and they showed their valor as well. The slaughter was great on both sides. For every Westerner the Imperial Army killed, the Western guards killed three Easterners. But all seemed in vain. However many holes were made in the Eastern line, twenty more Easterners rushed in to fill in the gap. As dawn broke, it was obvious the borders had been overrun. The only survivor of the West was Hamai, who also had killed more Easterners than anyone in his army; four hundred men he had slain that night. As soon as Hamai saw the last remaining

4

border guards being surrounded, he fled on horseback to inform Andiril of all that had transpired.

Hamai rode on horseback all morning and through into the evening. As first light was showing behind him the following morning, creeping over the mountaintops, he spotted the fortress of Andiril. It was surely a welcomed sight. The first thing noticed by Hamai would be the walls. The walls that surrounded Andiril's fortress were colossal, second only to Gūrond's. There were a couple of well-defended cities in the West, but they could not even begin to compare to the fortress of Andiril. The walls were seventy feet tall with the wall foundations going another twenty feet underground. The walls were fifteen feet thick, solid rock. The gates were made of the finest steel and opened outward instead of inward, making the gate harder to break open. The fortress itself was built at the base of a mountain range, so walls were needed on only three sides.

Walking up to Andiril, being physically tired and covered in blood, Hamai humbly bowed in adoration and asked to speak.

"What news have you from the border?" asked Andiril.

"The Imperial Army has overrun the frontier. They are advancing along the entire front as we speak to the frontier villages. With these villages taken, the Imperial Army will be able to establish a base with in our borders," replied Hamai who was anxiously awaiting Andiril's reply.

"How long before the army is ready?" asked Andiril.

"Not for another three days at least. The men from the outskirts of the kingdom are just arriving, and all the men have yet to be armed," stated Hamai.

"You have two days. Anytime sooner would be appreciated. Now go, Hamai, make ready the army."

With these orders, Hamai and his advisors went to get the army ready for battle. Just as Hamai was walking out of the throne room, Andiril called out to Hamai.

"Hamai!" shouted Andiril.

"Yes, my lord?" said Hamai, jogging back to Andiril.

"Go and keep an eye on the Imperial Army. Every morning I want you to report to me on what is happening," ordered Andiril. "Your advisors and lesser commanders can get the army ready by themselves."

"Yes, my lord. But how will I travel those great distances every day?" wondered Hamai. Even though the Western kingdom was far smaller than the East, distances between the fortress and villages were still vast—hundreds of kilometers.

"You won't. Take this diamond quill and blank tapestry. Every time you write on the tapestry, what you have written will then appear on this identical tapestry. I can also commune with you in the same way with this identical diamond quill," said Andiril, showing Hamai how it works.

"But how . . . ?" asked Hamai, stunned with bewilderment.

"My mother enchanted them," answered Andiril. "As you saw, the tapestry to which you are writing starts to glow, so you or I will be able to know that the other wishes to commune. Also, you should know that the messages will disappear in about thirty seconds from the time you finish writing. Now go, Hamai, and spy on the Imperial Army and await my orders."

"Yes, sir," replied Hamai.

Meanwhile, in Gūrond's citadel, Gūrond was talking with his top commander, Galdier. Galdier was the hero of the East. Among all Eastern mortals, he was the most skilled at sword and javelin. His battle tactics were also superior to anyone, even Gūrond and Andiril. Because of this, Galdier was the most valuable asset Gūrond had at his disposal, which also, undoubtedly, was why Galdier was the commander of the Imperial Army.

"What is the status of the campaign?" demanded Gūrond.

"Our army is advancing on every front taking every town and city as we go, slaying all women and children but forcing all able-bodied men into the Imperial Army, slaying those unable," reported Galdier.

"Very good," sneered Gūrond. "Go back and rejoin the army. At least twice a day I want a report from the front," demanded Gūrond, handing Galdier a spherical object. "When you wish to contact me, wave your hand over this three times. It is called a Telanris. After doing this, it will begin to glow. When the glowing stops, you may then talk through your Telanris to this one, which will always be at my side on this table next to my throne chair. When I need to contact you, your Telanris will start glowing; and through mine to yours, will I contact you. Now go."

"Yes, sir, I will return to the Imperial Army immediately," responded Galdier with the Telanris.

With every battle that was to follow, with every village that would be taken, the brutality and ruthlessness of the Imperial Army would show forth. The entire army would eventually become bent on the total destruction of the West. From now on, the Imperial Army would go into battle not planning to spare any civilians or garrison men they would encounter.

Back in the West, Andiril was at the Temple of the Priestesses taking on counsel with his mother, Gwentythe.

"Why wouldn't my father take heed to your warnings, O Priestess Mother?" asked Andiril.

"He was blinded by the deceit which came from the mouth of Gūrond. As I recall, you were deceived as well until the attacks started twenty years ago," replied Gwentythe.

"Am I doomed then, in that I am too much like my father?" cried out Andiril.

"No. Being an Immortal, you are not bound by the faults of your father and can choose your own fate. No longer listen to Gūrond. Rather, listen to yourself and listen to me. Take heed of all my wisdom. Do this with whatever you may gain from Above or Below and you may very well succeed. Do not be hasty, but clothe yourself with the robe of patience and drench yourself in the rains of my wisdom," encouraged Gwentythe, putting her hand on the side of Andiril's head, caressing it.

"What about Gūrond? Are you to share your wisdom with him as well?" wondered Andiril.

"No. I am not obligated to share any more of my wisdom with him. The wisdom I have is mine to share with whomever I wish.

Because of him, you are now at war and do not rule the kingdom of your father. Because of him, the world may be covered with a lasting darkness. Giving him more wisdom than he already has would not be beneficial towards anyone," replied Gwentythe. "All that can save him now is the wisdom given to him from Above or Below. Now go back to your throne room. It is almost time for your daily worship by the mortals."

As Andiril bowed to Gwentythe, he took her hand and kissed it. As soon as he kissed her hand, he said to her, "May you ever dwell in the land, and may your wisdom benefit all who hear it." Then he rose and walked to his throne room.

As he sat down on his throne, Andiril noticed the room was full of the Second Created. Just as soon as he was in his chair, they all prostrated themselves on the throne room floor, which was covered with designs and murals just as the walls and ceiling were. As the mortals were on the ground, they were saying, "All hail our Immortal, who looks after and cares for us. May he rule over us, his servants, with wisdom and justice. All hail!" This worshiping went on for some time with various other phrases. After this was over, all the mortals gave Andiril gifts as was required. Each gave according to his profession. Farmers gave generous portions of their crops (harvesting in this world occurred weekly as all the land was suitable for farming and extremely efficient; there was also no "winter" season); herders gave multiple animals; blacksmiths gave elaborately decorated swords and ornately designed armor; tailors gave clothes they had made by hand from cotton, silk, and wool; and the majority of the people gave things of wealth such as gold or jewelry.

The worshiping of an Immortal occurred once a day while the gift giving only happened once a week as a sign of gratitude from the mortals to the Immortals. The gifts were presented

9

individually, and Andiril had to bless every single one. If a gift was deemed unworthy, the mortal who brought it must return it and bring yet another gift that must be blessed as well. If the second time the gift was rejected, the mortal must bring yet another gift; but the third time a gift was rejected, that mortal's life was declared forfeit and, depending on Andiril's mood, was either killed or used as slave labor.

There were certain guidelines a mortal must abide by when presenting a gift no matter what that gift was. The gift if a piece of clothing, armor, or an animal must appear perfect, without blemish. If a piece of clothing or armor, it must fit Andiril perfectly; and since everyone had Andiril's measurements, this was without excuse. If a farmer presented crops, they must be at least a basketful (all farmers were assigned a basket from Andiril himself) and some of the best from the weekly harvest. All those who gave valuables like gold or jewelry had equal wealth, so if one mortal gave less than the rest, that meant they were holding back from Andiril. All of the above guidelines must be followed exactly, and those who did not follow were not tolerated. For the most part, everyone did adhere to them, but occasionally someone did not.

There was one occasion when a certain mortal named Daldier presented to Andiril some money. When counted, Daldier's gift was five pounds short of gold. But because Andiril showed much compassion toward mortals and being in a good mood, he allowed Daldier to go and bring the rest of the gold. If it had been Gūrond who had been shorted, he would have sent Daldier to a javelin-throwing squad to be impaled. Or if Gūrond was feeling rather merciful, he might send Daldier to an iron or gold mine. He would be working twenty-four hours a day every day with a couple of five-minute breaks each day. Those who were sent to work in these mines, however, usually died within the first three months because of the strenuous working conditions.

Back at one of the towns Gūrond's forces had captured, his commanders were conferring on what course of action should be taken next in the conquest of the West. Gūrond's top commander, Galdier, told the others his strategy.

"You two take one-quarter of the army and head northwest," said Galdier to two commanders on his left. "You two take another quarter of the army and head southwest," he said to two commanders on his right. "And I will take the rest of the army and head straight across towards the fortress of Andiril. As we are all advancing, do not forget Gūrond's commands—capture every village, force all able-bodied men into the army, kill everyone else," directed Galdier. "We shall meet here," said Galdier, pointing to a spot on the map in front of him, "in order to attack Andiril's fortress full force." As the other commanders were leaving the tent, Galdier took the Telanris out of his pack and started waving his hand over it to update Gūrond on the situation.

"I have sent troops to the north and south. I am heading straight for the fortress of Andiril. We will meet each other for a combined siege." Just as soon as Galdier was done waving his hand over the ball and starting to speak, Gūrond's Telanris started glowing, and the message appeared through Galdier's Telanris to Gūrond's.

In response, Gūrond said, "Excellent. I sense that the end of the war is near, and then I can finally face my cowardly brother and be rid of him. Until then, Galdier, you know what to do." With that, each Telanris ceased glowing, signifying each was done talking to the other, and Galdier placed the Telanris back in his pack.

CHAPTER 2

 ūrond's Imperial Army continued to advance on all fronts, capturing town after town. The couple of walled cities that were left put up the greatest resistance and caused the most casualties to the Imperial Army. The northern force had the easiest time as they encountered no walled cities and little resistance, while the southern force had to capture a walled city as its first objective. Even though the southern force sustained heavy casualties—about a thousand total—it made up for this loss with the able-bodied men who were forced into the Imperial Army. The only major resistance the northern encountered was at the last village it took, sustaining minimal casualties.

Meanwhile, in the center of the excitement was Galdier's force consisting of half of the entire Imperial Army. Galdier's force sustained the least number of casualties of any of the Imperial forces. His vast force completely surrounded the unwalled village it came to and, first unleashing a deadly volley from the catapults, utterly annihilated the village. After the volley from the catapults, the Imperial Army ran into the city from every side, completely outflanking the entire city. As with every town that was taken, the slaughter was great. Every living soul in the city was slaughtered—women, children, and every last garrison man who survived the volley from the catapults. The bodies piled up by the thousands with no less than seven hundred bodies at the smallest village. However, the greatest and most brutal massacre would take place at the next city, where Galdier's force and the slightly weakened southern force would come together and attack the walled city as one.

The town garrisons at this city were the largest force encountered since the initial invasion by the Imperial Army. The night before the siege began, Galdier took the mystic Telanris from his pack to update Gūrond.

"We are encamped outside the last southern city in the Western kingdom. The northern force is waiting at the last northern village so we can march full force to the last city and finally to Andiril's fortress," said Galdier into the ball.

Gūrond responded back, "Very good. This campaign is going exceedingly well. I would guess in a couple of days, you will be at Andiril's fortress, and then I can finally meet him and destroy him. Then I can finally claim what is rightfully mine—all the land between the two fortresses. Continue as has been planned. When you reach the last city, wave your hand over the ball and hold it in front of you so that I can see the city fall myself," replied Gūrond.

"Yes, my lord."

With that, the Telanris ceased glowing.

Back at Andiril's fortress, Andiril was talking with Hamai.

"My lord, Gūrond's forces are at the last southern city. They have it completely surrounded. Is there no hope left?"

"Why do you have so little faith? In a short while I will come face-to-face with my treacherous brother, then all will be settled. As soon as I am done with his evil spirit, peace will be brought back, and all will be as it once was," responded Andiril. "Now go, Hamai, go to the last northern city and take another city garrison with you. Hold out for as long as you can. As soon as the enemy enters the city, I want you to return to my fortress and prepare for the final siege. Then when I return from facing Gūrond, peace will be restored, and the land will have one ruler again."

"Yes, my lord. Long live Andiril and the Western kingdom!" With that, Hamai bowed to Andiril and left for the last northern city.

In the fortress of Gūrond, one of his top courtmen informed him of the statistical part of the campaign. Humbly bowing then asking to speak, he then read from a scroll.

"Since the invasion, six unwalled towns have been captured, with none remaining. Two walled cities have been captured, with one remaining. Of the 675,000 troops, 35,000 were lost on the night of the invasion in return for killing the entire frontier garrison of the West. We have lost 750 more men in the sieges of the walled towns, but with all the men we have forced into the army, we are back to 675,000 strong. To date, one million Western townsfolk have been killed. However, some have managed to escape."

"How many, couple dozen perhaps?" asked Gūrond.

"It is estimated as many as 100,000 townsfolk have escaped the slaughter."

"What! How could this happen?" demanded Gūrond, completely furious that some Westerners escaped his genocide.

"Apparently Andiril managed to evacuate three southern villages while we were battling the frontier garrisons," replied the courtman.

Somewhat satisfied to hear it was not the fault of his army that so many villagers escaped the carnage, Gūrond said, "At least the army will be able to have more fun when they take the fortress after I do away with Andiril." Gūrond sat back on his throne with a devilish smirk on his face.

Back in Andiril's fortress, Andiril began writing on the tapestry with the diamond quill to commune with Hamai at the last northern city. "What preparations are you taking for the inevitable siege ahead?" Soon after he started writing, Hamai's tapestry started glowing. After unfolding the tapestry, Andiril's message appeared on Hamai's. In response, Hamai wrote, "I am placing two garrisons outside the city and leaving one inside. As soon as the garrison in the city starts battling with the Imperial Army, I will return to your fortress, my lord."

"Good. And upon your return to my fortress, you and I will begin planning the defense of my stronghold," replied Andiril. With that, the discussion was over, and Hamai carefully folded up the tapestry and placed it in his pack.

Sometime later, Andiril went to the Temple of the Priestesses to consult his mother, Gwentythe. Humbly bowing before her, Andiril then began to ask of her wisdom.

"What news have you, O Priestess Mother?"

"I looked into the future, and I saw pain . . . suffering . . . death. But hope remains with you, Andiril. As soon as Gūrond's forces start besieging your fortress, Gūrond will be taken either Above or Below, then you will be taken to the place he was not. I have also seen that you will be taken to the place he was not one day after he is taken. One day after you are taken, you and Gūrond shall meet at the tower on the mountains. Whoever returns from the tower alive will then rule all the land until his five hundred years are over. The day Gūrond will start the siege is unknown. Only the Unknown knows."

"All I can do now is wait patiently and see to the defenses of the fortress," stated Andiril.

"If you do not wish for the sun to forever go down in the West, you must defeat Gūrond. Only then will your kingdom be safe, and only then will you rule all the land," warned Gwentythe.

"Does Gūrond know that his siege on my fortress is linked to going Above or Below?" asked Andiril.

"No. And he most likely will not know until that time comes. Now go and make haste with your preparations that are needed. Time is running short," encouraged Gwentythe. After bowing to Gwentythe once more, Andiril left the temple.

Just before dawn broke, the siege of the last southern city started. The number of large rocks hurled by the hundred catapults was vast. The other hundred catapults along with all the siege towers were with the northern force. The combined army of Galdier's force and the southern force had completely surrounded the walled city. The large rocks launched by the catapults were hitting the walls of the city from every direction. Having no rams with which to ram the gate of the city, all the army could do now was wait for a breach in the wall, then pour in to overwhelm the defenders. Having no way to fight back until a breach had occurred, the defenders could only sit and wait to be massacred. Knowing this, the defending garrison was trembling with fear. Then, after some time of pounding away at the city walls, the Imperial Army was finally granted access to the city within. The whole northern portion of the wall collapsed, with the rest of the wall quickly following. As soon as the northern section of the wall started to fall, the Imperial Army ran toward the wall. Then, when it finally fell to the ground with a great dust cloud proceeding from the fall, the army poured into the city from the huge gap given to them. Because of the sheer size of the army, it was impossible for the defending garrison to fend off the Imperial Army. Nearly half of the Imperial Army was able to get inside the city, while the other half got in through the southern breach. With such odds against them, the defending garrison was simply crushed from both sides. The total number of dead, including those who lived in the city, was fifty thousand. Fifteen thousand of those killed had been part of the city garrison while thirty-five thousand had been those who lived in the city. The only casualties the Imperial Army sustained were one hundred dead. After this battle, there was no one to force into the army; all had been slain.

Back in the East, Gūrond was planning the last phase of his campaign against the West with his top advisors.

"What course of action do you think we should take next?" asked Gūrond to all his advisors standing around his chair. After conferring with each other, they came up with a logical plan.

"We think the siege of the last northern city should begin immediately followed soon after by the siege of Andiril's fortress," stated one of Gūrond's advisors.

"The siege of the last northern city will begin as soon as possible," said Gūrond. "However, I have a feeling that besieging Andiril's fortress is somehow connected with the time which I will be taken either Above or Below. Therefore, my army will make camp outside the fortress. The army will stay encamped until I give the command to attack. Hopefully, the enemy will send out whatever forces they have conscripted so that my army may defeat it before the siege begins."

"Yes, sir."

With that, Gūrond's advisors bowed to Gūrond and left the throne room.

After his advisors had left the room, Gūrond took the Telanris beside his throne chair and waved his hand over it. Gūrond then spoke into the ball. "What plans are you taking for the final destruction of the West?" asked Gūrond.

Soon after Gūrond started speaking, Galdier's Telanris started glowing. Galdier then waved his hand over the ball and listened to the message coming through to him. Galdier then sent a reply. "Soon after taking the last city, the army was going to attack the fortress."

"No. After taking the last city, make camp around the fortress. Stay there until I say. Be alert for an attack from Andiril's fortress garrison sallying forth."

"As you wish, sir." With that, both Telanris stopped glowing, and the conversation was over.

Back in the West, Hamai was preparing the last city for the imminent attack by the Imperial Army.

"Take two-thirds of the garrison and make camp outside the city. Stay there, and when the army of the East comes, hold as long as you can. You and your men will not be allowed back into the city," said Hamai to an inferior-in-rank commander.

"Yes, sir. We will fight to the death for the West!" said the commander to Hamai.

"The West is forever grateful for your contribution," encouraged Hamai, embracing the lesser commander.

As two-thirds of the city garrison made its way outside the city, Hamai commanded the last third of the garrison to be just behind the main gate of the city. Hamai stayed with the garrison inside the city so when the Imperial Army broke through, he could escape through one of the lesser gates of the city. As night fell, Hamai could hear the machines of war rolling onward beyond the horizon toward the city. The rest of the garrison could hear this as well, and all wondered when the battle would begin, causing much anxiety throughout the garrison. All night every one of the garrison men only thought of the slaughter ahead, nothing else. The thought lingered over everyone, even the townsfolk, like a cloud with thunder and lightning. After several hours, Hamai got word that the torches of the enemy had been spotted in the distance. The time was drawing ever nearer.

CHAPTER 3

 s dawn broke, all the garrison men could see the encampment of the Imperial Army. Though not close enough to start the siege, it was close enough to let everyone know that today was the day. It was just a matter of when the Imperial Army wished to start the inevitable battle. Hamai was continuing to make the necessary preparations for the siege the best he could. As Hamai was preparing for the inevitable battle ahead, Galdier noticed all the garrison men outside the last city of the West.

"So they wish to die outside the city, eh? Well, we shall grant their request," Galdier said to himself. "March forward!" he shouted. As soon as he said this, all the men and machines of war made their way toward the city. Galdier then took out the Telanris from his pack, waved his hand over it, and held it above his head to let Gūrond see the entire battle.

One-third of the remaining garrison men inside the city Hamai ordered to stand on top of the walls surrounding the main gate with javelins to throw at the attackers. The remaining two-thirds were commanded to wait just behind the gate. Hamai concentrated so much on getting the city ready for the siege that some time passed until Hamai noticed that the Imperial Army was moving. When he saw this, Hamai hastily ran around saying anything to uplift the men and encourage them, as well as making any final orders. Then, out of the silence, several men shouted, "Catapults!" Within a couple of seconds of this, massive boulders came raining down on the walls of the city. Some hit short of the walls, crushing the men standing outside of the city, not moving despite the boulders falling on them. They just stood firm waiting to battle the Imperial Army. Those boulders that hit the walls crushed some of the men on top while others on top of the walls fell to their deaths as parts of the walls collapsed.

Suddenly, the aim of the catapults changed, and the boulders began flying at the gate itself. It didn't take long before the gate was obliterated. Soon after, Galdier gave the order to charge; and with that, 340,000 men ran toward the city gate. When the overwhelming mass of men was about 30 yards away from the walls Hamai shouted, "Unleash the javelins!" and a plethora of javelins came down upon the first few rows of the charging men, with minimal effect. Then, the front line of the Imperial Army met with the front line of the garrison men, full force. Shield met sword, sword met spear, and spear met shield. The carnage was great, but the savagery was greater. In many instances during the battle, instead of using weapons to kill, weapons were thrown down; and people on both sides were beaten to death with kicks and punches. More often than not, it was a Westerner fighting in this way. Such was the emotion and despair of the Westerners. They knew of the brutality of the Imperial Army. They knew of the hundreds of thousands, perhaps millions, of mortals slain by the Imperial Army. Their adrenaline was rushing so, that many times members of the Western garrison were found fighting missing a limb.

However, despite the valor and courage of the garrison men, they were no match for an army ten times its size. Those men unlucky enough to be outside the walls kept dropping like flies even though a great number of the Imperial Army had also fallen. As all this was going on, those men on top of the walls kept hurling javelins at the Imperial Army until all of the javelins had been thrown. Much to their dismay, many of the javelins were thrown back to those who had thrown them, some hitting their mark, others just flying over the walls. Soon the last of garrison men outside the walls were killed, and the Imperial Army started pouring into the city through the broken gate. As soon as the Imperial Army met with those inside the city, Hamai hastily slipped away through a gate at the opposite side of the city. Hamai used the forest behind the city for cover, and before night fell, Hamai was safely (for the time being) back at Andiril's fortress. At this point, Galdier placed the Telanris back in his pack and had stumbled upon Hamai's tapestry and diamond quill, which he also placed in his pack.

Hamai walked into Andiril's throne room.

"What news do you bring?" asked Andiril as soon as he noticed Hamai.

"The city is taken. All the men were lost. We killed many of the enemy, however. Yet with every battle, it seems that the Imperial Army is getting bigger, not smaller. How can this be?" wondered Hamai.

"After every city or village was taken, every able-bodied male is forced into the Imperial Army. You were fighting against some of your own countrymen," replied Andiril.

"Oh, woe of woes! Horror of horrors! My fellow countrymen deserved not to die. 'Tis the men of the invading Imperial Army that deserve death. When will vengeance be cast upon them? When will the lives of our soldiers be avenged? When will justice be done unto them? Will the Ruler of the East and his subjects ever be judged and cast into the Abyss? Oh, Unknown, hear me and vindicate those who fight for freedom and for the light!" cried out Hamai, quite passionately and heartfelt.

"Be not troubled, Hamai. Yes, they were forced into the Imperial Army, and yes, our soldiers killed them; but because it was against their will, this sin will not be held against those countrymen forced into the enemy army. Nor will anything be held against those who killed them. Their eventual destination will be the same as yours." After hearing these things, Hamai was very much comforted. However, he did still resent killing his fellow countrymen.

"Thank you, my lord." After bowing, Hamai walked from the throne room to his quarters in the fortress.

Back at the newly conquered Western city, Galdier wished to commune with Gūrond on what had transpired just recently. Reaching into his pack, he pulled out the Telanris. Then Galdier proceeded to speak into the Telanris.

"The last Western city has fallen as you saw through the Telanris. The sun shall soon forever set in the West. We will march for Andiril's fortress immediately," said Galdier.

"Yes. Proceed to the fortress as soon as possible. However, when you arrive at the fortress, make camp and stay there, not attacking till I order you to," commanded Gūrond.

"Yes, my lord. One more thing, sir, I happened to find an enchanted tapestry and diamond quill. What would it have been used for? I wonder," asked Galdier.

"These were used between Hamai and Andiril to commune with each other much the same way we use the Telanris to commune between ourselves. They may be of great use to us in the near future," replied Gūrond. "Now go and do as I have commanded you."

With that, each Telanris ceased to glow. Galdier placed his back in the pack, and Gūrond set his on the table next to his chair.

After communing with Gūrond, Galdier ordered all commanders to his quarters. Galdier then told all commanders what Gūrond had told him.

"We will do the will of our lord, but I wonder, why wait at the fortress gates? Why not take it the first chance we get?" asked one of Galdier's commanders.

"Because it was our lord who commanded it. Do not forget your place, mortal. We are to always obey our Immortal's orders. Or maybe I should inform Gūrond of your questioning his authority?" replied Galdier.

"No. That's all the answer I need," said the commander, trembling with fear at the thought of Gūrond ever finding out he questioned his lord.

"Good. Tomorrow morning we will move out towards Andiril's fortress," said Galdier. With that, all commanders left Galdier's quarters and returned to their troops.

The next morning, the wheels of war rolled forward toward Andiril's fortress followed by the troops in the Imperial Army. As this was happening, Andiril was in the Temple of the Priestesses consulting the wisdom of Gwentythe.

"What do you foresee, O Great Priestess?" asked Andiril, bowing as he asked.

"I see all the machines and soldiers of the enemy advancing towards your massive fortress, Andiril. However, because Gūrond knows that the siege of your fortress will bring about his time going Above or Below, he will not attack right away. His vast army will make camp around the fortress," informed Gwentythe.

"The end is near at hand. And though I know not the outcome or where I am going, either Above or Below, I will trust in the Unknown as well as myself. Even as I stand outnumbered, outmanned, outflanked, I will stand my ground till the death. If I shall die, I will rejoice in becoming one with the Unknown and see him in all his glory. If I shall live and my adversary die, I will rejoice in him forever living in unrelenting torment. Therefore, whatever happens, I will rejoice," stated Andiril.

"Well said, my dear Andiril. Go and prepare for the siege which will happen in the near future. And with your positive attitude, the tide may very well turn," encouraged Gwentythe.

"Thank you, Mother. May your foresight and wisdom ever bless you and those around you." After saying this, Andiril left the temple to return to his throne room.

Back in the East, Gūrond's subjects were coming to Gūrond's fortress to worship him and bring the weekly gifts due him. His throne room was filled to the brim with the Second Created from

Gūrond's lands. Even though Gūrond's fortress was larger than Andiril's, all the Second Created could not fit in the vast fortress let alone the throne room. Then all at once, everyone prostrated themselves toward Gūrond and repeated phrases to Gūrond that had been said toward Andiril by his subjects. After this, everyone brought their gifts to Gūrond one by one all according to their profession. All was going well until a farmer brought some of his crop, and much of it was going brown. Unknown to Gūrond, the farmer had two baskets: one for Gūrond and one for the bad plants of his crop he had found. In a rush to get to Gūrond, the farmer mistakenly grabbed the bad basket instead of Gūrond's basket. Gūrond was furious.

"How dare you bring me this crop that you should have fed to the pigs! To the mines with you! May you at least profit me until your death," said Gūrond, feeling rather merciful that day. Not saying anything, the farmer was led out of the throne room to the closest mine. When everyone had given their gifts, everything was taken and stored away in the back of the fortress. There was a room for all the food, a gigantic vault for all the gold, and a huge closet for all the armor and fine clothes given to Gūrond from the Second Created. After the worshiping had ended and all the gifts stored away, Gūrond's advisors walked into his throne room and humbly bowed.

"What news do you bring?" asked Gūrond.

"We bring word that the Imperial Army is at Andiril's fortress and making camp around it. They are waiting for orders," informed Gūrond's top advisor.

"Very good. Now be gone."

"Yes, my lord." With that, all Gūrond's advisors left the throne room. When they had gone, Gūrond waved his hand over the Telanris and proceeded to speak.

"I have just gotten word that you have reached the fortress and are making camp."

"Yes, sir," replied Galdier. "We are at the fortress and awaiting your orders."

"Stay there and do not attack. The end is near, and I need to be prepared. Wait for my order to attack," said Gūrond. After this, each Telanris stopped glowing.

Back in the West, Hamai and all the garrison men at Andiril's fortress looked from the fortress walls to see, to their horror, the Imperial Army making camp around the fortress. After seeing this, Hamai ran to Andiril's throne room and bowed before his master.

"What is it, Hamai? And what is troubling you that you should look so worried?" wondered Andiril.

"The whole of the Imperial Army is right outside our door. They are making camp around your fortress. Will the siege begin tomorrow morning?" asked Hamai.

"No," responded Andiril. "Gūrond needs to make himself ready for our fight. What he is doing to prepare for it I do not know. What I do know is I do not fear death, and neither should you. For if we should die, we will live in everlasting paradise. Should the enemy die, they will live in eternal hell, beyond the Second Created Netherworld," said Andiril.

29

"Thank you, my lord," responded Hamai, having been very much comforted by Andiril's words of wisdom.

"Oh, one more thing, Hamai. The secret weapon some of the men have been working on is almost ready for use against the Imperial Army. In a day or two it should be complete, then all we have to do is wait for the enemy army to attack."

After hearing this, Hamai returned to the fortress walls and did his best to encourage the garrison men with him. The number of garrison men ready to protect the fortress was 175,000; still nothing compared to 675,000 Easterners but still triple the number that had defended the previous city. As the men continued to look out unto the great host of Easterners, they noticed all the catapults and siege towers. Victory seemed even further from grasp than it had before, if any Westerners even thought there was any hope to begin with. Hamai looked around at all the garrison men and noticed how discouraged and without hope they all appeared. He took it upon himself being the commander to encourage his fellow Westerners, so he said in a loud voice, "Friends, brothers, be not dismayed. They may have numbers on their side, but of what use are they? Wars are not won by these things alone. We have courage and bravery. We need to protect our families and homes, and most importantly our king and Immortal. Our king will be right here with us. What about theirs? The Easterner's king is a thousand miles away hiding in his fortress. Fear not, for an Immortal can do much worse to you than a mortal can."

Hamai's speech helped some, but many were still depressed at the odds against them.

CHAPTER 4

Before the final siege was to begin, Gwentythe called Gūrond and Andiril to her temple.

"I foresee that the end is near. I foresee you both going Above or Below, and I now know which of you is to go where," said Gwentythe.

"Where am I going, Mother? Tell me now!" demanded Gūrond, hastily and wide-eyed.

"No. I cannot tell either of you where you are going. The Unknown wants it to remain a surprise for the both of you."

"So am I going Above then?" asked Gūrond.

"I can say no more about this," said Gwentythe.

"You are most definitely not going Above, for what does the Unknown have to say to you but 'Be gone, away from me, doer of iniquity!'" stated Andiril toward Gūrond.

"Your insolence towards me and your false ideas about the Unknown are your weaknesses. The Unknown has blessed my invasion, and my army is completely surrounding you now because the Unknown is with those who take initiative. He is no friend of cowards such as yourself," sneered Gūrond.

"Stop this, you two! You both know nothing of the Unknown. Soon, however, one of you shall meet him and know his true intentions soon enough. Now go, out of my sight!" demanded Gwentythe.

As Andiril and Gūrond were leaving, they stopped in the hallway and talked a little while longer.

"Gūrond, we can save a lot of lives if we end the fighting now. What if I give you authority over three-quarters of the entire kingdom and I reside over just one-quarter? What say you to that?" offered Andiril.

"You never were much of a diplomat, nor a negotiator, so I must say no. I will accept nothing less than the entire kingdom. Now let me give an offer to you. Give me control over the entire kingdom and you shall be my personal servant. If you accept, I will no longer plan to besiege your fortress. If you truly want to save lives, you dare not reject it," replied Gūrond.

"I cannot accept such an offer as I am the elder of the two of us and true heir to the entire kingdom."

"Very well, Andiril." Gūrond started to leave, then turned around and said one final word. "If you were the kind and merciful ruler you believe yourself to be, you would know of sacrifice and would have gladly given up anything for your mortals." As Gūrond turned and started to walk away, he said, "I look forward to killing you soon."

Andiril just stood there watching Gūrond leave, wondering how someone as heartless as Gūrond would know anything about mercy or kindness. Yet in his heart, Andiril realized Gūrond had some truth in what he had just said. After Gūrond was out of sight, Andiril returned to his throne room and Gūrond returned to his.

As Andiril entered his throne room, he noticed Gwentythe was standing right next to his throne chair.

"I remember enchanting this tapestry and diamond quill as well as those you gave to Hamai," recalled Gwentythe. Andiril walked to and sat in his throne. "I also recall enchanting those two gauntlets Endiril gave to you and Gūrond. Oh how I wish I never had done such a thing. No matter."

"What really brings you here? Never have I ever seen you anywhere but in the temple," asked Andiril.

"I have some words of wisdom for you. I dare not tell Gūrond. You know of the other gauntlet how it never reached Gūrond. Well, it is hidden in the tower on the mountains. The Unknown hid it there. He also placed there a ring that he made himself. In this way, one Immortal will have the power to conquer the other."

"So I will be able to defeat Gūrond with this ring even if he finds the second gauntlet?" wondered Andiril.

"That I was not told. I was only told what was hidden, where it was hidden, and the powers which I have just told you. Use this information wisely, keep it for yourself, and victory will ultimately be yours." With that, Gwentythe left Andiril alone to meditate to the wisdom given him.

Back in the East, Gūrond was consulting his advisors on what course of action should be taken next.

"We think that since you have delayed besieging this long, you should wait even longer. We think you have waited because you were worried about beginning the siege and not going to the place you think you should go," suggested an advisor.

"Interesting. You are of course wrong as usual. I don't even know why I have any advisors in the first place. Oh yeah, I remember, my father had you in his court, so it would be rude to kill you all as I wanted to. What I plan to do is ride up to Andiril's fortress and suggest we end this war right there in front of his fortress in a duel to the death," replied Gūrond.

"Yes, my lord. Shall we get your steed ready?"

"Yes. Tomorrow if Andiril is any sort of man, he will come out to meet me, and I will fight him and kill him."

Just as Gūrond said, the next day, he arrived at his army's encampment surrounding Andiril's fortress. Hamai looked out from the fortress walls and saw Gūrond arrive at the Imperial Army's encampment. He could tell it was Gūrond because of the horse he rode on along with the overly ornate armor he wore. Only those of importance ride horses. And only Immortals wear full-suit armor. Galdier walked up to Gūrond.

"Galdier, go as my messenger to Andiril and give him this message: 'Come out and fight me, brother, so we may end this war now. We will fight to the death and for the right of ruling the entire kingdom.'" After Gūrond was done telling Galdier what to say, Galdier was sent to the fortress gate.

"I come bearing word for your Immortal from Gūrond the Great, Ruler of the East," stated Galdier.

Remarkably, without any argument, the gatekeeper yelled, "Open the gate!" Galdier walked through the massive gate and proceeded directly to Andiril's throne room toward the back of the citadel. Galdier entered Andiril's throne room, walked up to the throne, and waited for Andiril to speak.

"What news do you bring?" asked Andiril, noticing with agitation that Galdier didn't bow.

"My master, Gūrond the Great, has a message for you: 'Come and fight me, brother, in order to end the war now. Let us fight to the death and for the right of ruling the whole kingdom.'"

Andiril was not thrilled in hearing this and almost immediately said, "You come here and refuse to bow to an Immortal. You come on behalf of Gūrond and with much arrogance. I must reject this offer. Leave now before I don't let you," replied Andiril. With that, Galdier left the throne room. Hamai walked up to Andiril.

"Let us give our guest a goodbye present," ordered Andiril. Hamai knew exactly what he meant.

"Yes, my lord," said Hamai. With that, he went and ordered the newly created bows distributed among the men on the walls along with a quiver of arrows for each man. The bows themselves were very long. Since the research on this weapon began, Andiril noticed that the bigger the bow, the farther the arrow can be shot, so the final bows he came up with were four and a half feet tall.

The bows and quivers were distributed among the men on the walls as soon as was possible. When they were ready, Galdier was just about to inform Gūrond on the proposal.

"Andiril rejected the offer, sire," stated Galdier. Just as he had finished saying this, Gūrond noticed a dark cloud, or what he thought was a cloud, coming toward the Imperial Army. Then it suddenly descended onto the front ranks of the army, with those men screaming out in agony. Gūrond at once knew it to be some type of new weapon.

"I see that. The garrison men are attacking the army with some long projectile."

As he said this, Galdier turned around, noticing all the men at the front falling dead from the arrows puncturing the weak spots in the armor.

"That's impossible. No man can throw that far," said Galdier, dumbfounded.

"They are not throwing anything. They are shooting it," replied Gūrond. Being an Immortal, he caught on very fast to this new weapon of warfare.

"This weapon may give the enemy an advantage. Attack at once!" ordered Gūrond.

"Catapults, fire at will! Siege towers and infantry to the walls!" yelled Galdier.

Just as the first boulders from the catapults were hitting the gate, Gūrond disappeared from atop his steed.

Gūrond at once found himself standing in the midst of a sun-soaked field. He looked around and was utterly struck at what he saw. He was standing outside an immense citadel. Around the citadel walls was a seemingly never-ending field of the purest, most perfect green grass Gūrond had ever seen. Gūrond then turned around and noticed the walls surrounding the citadel. The walls were a mile high and stretched well beyond the horizon in either direction! The gate into the city then opened. The gate itself was one thousand five hundred feet high! Gūrond slowly walked through the gate. As he did, he noticed the street he was walking on was made of emeralds and precious stones. There was but one road in this citadel of heaven, and it went straight to the central castle. The castle itself was five hundred stories high, a perfect square, with each side a mile long. A moat went all the way around the castle filled with water clear as glass with a drawbridge leading directly into the castle. Gūrond walked through the drawbridge and into the castle. He walked into the main hall, which was immense, five times as big as Gūrond's own throne room. He continued walking until, through the incredible light all around, he made out the throne itself. Gūrond proceeded to walk up to the throne and did something no one had ever seen an Immortal do before—he bowed. He bowed down at the foot of the throne now fully grasping where he was—before the very throne of heaven.

"To your feet, Gūrond, son of Endiril," said the Unknown from the throne. "I have some information to give to you. Information on something you have been searching for since it was lost. The gauntlet you so long for is in the tower on the mountains. With this in your possession, you will have the strength to defeat Andiril. With this new strength, you will be able to wield this sword, the sword of heaven. You cannot wield it on your own strength."

As the Unknown said this, two angelic servants brought the sword forth. These two servants looked somewhat similar to

Immortals. These beings, however, were taller, with pure white hair and pure white robes. They seemed to glide over the floor and yet had no wings. The sword was the most impressive, beautiful weapon Gūrond had ever laid eyes on. Forged with a heavenly metal Gūrond was not familiar with, it was able to cut through any armor or weapon. The blade was double-sided, and the handle was studded with the same precious stones and emeralds he had noticed on the street. The two servants strapped the now-sheathed sword on Gūrond's back.

"Now go, Gūrond, and claim the other gauntlet." As soon as the Unknown said this, Gūrond was in the forest below the tower on the mountains. He then started his long trek up to the tower.

Back at Andiril's fortress, the siege was continuing with Galdier commanding the army of the East. Galdier noticed to his displeasure that the catapults had minimal effect on the incredibly thick walls of the fortress.

"The gate, you fools! Aim the catapults at the gate!" commanded Galdier, hoping that the catapults would have better luck attacking the gate. Meanwhile, the siege towers were progressing ever closer to the walls. Each of the forty siege towers was as tall as the fortress walls. Being so massive, each tower took four hundred fifty men to move. The towers continued their journey to the walls all night with the catapults still blasting away at the gate. Right before dawn, the gate finally gave way from all the stones pounding against it, and it collapsed backward into the fortress. Soon after the towers reached the walls, men came pouring through the gate and the siege towers as well. As this was happening, the sun started to rise, and Andiril was taken away.

Andiril looked around at where he was. It wasn't what he had expected. The ground appeared as black as darkness with pillars of smoke rising forth from it. He looked up, and it looked as if this accursed place was between two seemingly infinitely high cliffs. He looked to either side, and he noticed in the far-off distance were fires burning, but unlike any fires Andiril or anybody in the land of the living had ever seen. The fires here were white and blue and reached upward to the highest of heights. Then he looked forward and noticed a building that fit in nicely with the surrounding landscape. Andiril walked toward the building scanning the surrounding bleak and barren land. As he made his way toward it, Andiril noticed glowing red eyes gazing at him. Then creatures came forth from the darkness, hunched over as if crippled and black as coal with short coarse hairs covering their entire body. Andiril was starting to get a little worried as more and more of these grotesque monsters started appearing out of nowhere. However, these beasts of the underworld made no hostile moves toward Andiril; they only kept staring and growling and drooling profusely. Andiril walked into the building and followed the main hall till he got to the end of the hall. Having nowhere else to go, he turned right. At the end of this hallway was a door. Andiril opened it, and inside was a fireplace at the far right side of the room. Above the fireplace was an inscription. Andiril walked closer to get a better look. It said,

Against each other you have an equal stand,

More strength can be had by the power of your hand,

Look in the tower that on the mountains stand,

In a protective glove there's strength yet in the Emerald Sword

is the perfect man.

After reading this, Andiril instantly found himself at the base of the mountain where the tower was located. Andiril started the long trek up the mountain to the tower.

As Andiril was making his way up to the tower, Gūrond was feverishly searching the tower in order to find the second glove he lusted after. He went from room to room, every single room on every single floor, not wavering in his determination to at last be able to defeat his brother. It came about that when Gūrond entered the second to last room on the top floor, he saw what appeared to be an altar. He walked toward it. As he got closer, he realized that something was lying on top of it. Could it be his long-coveted gauntlet? Just the thought of it might actually being there on the altar gave Gūrond an adrenaline rush, and he bolted toward the altar. Halfway to the altar, he noticed that the object lying atop the altar was indeed the other gauntlet. At last! This only encouraged Gūrond to run all the faster in order to claim it. He stopped right in front of the altar and looked upon the gauntlet as a husband looks upon his bride for the first time. He most carefully lifted up the gauntlet and held it for a while, as if studying it. He did not realize the silver ring laying on the altar underneath the gauntlet. Then, he put his left hand into the gauntlet very gently. As soon as it was on, both gauntlets glowed bright colors: green, blue, yellow, red. Gūrond felt something, something wonderful. He felt invincible. To test this new strength, he grabbed the handle of the sword on his back. The sword that took two angelic beings to carry and place on his back, Gūrond unsheathed with one hand! Stunned by his new-found strength, Gūrond just stood there for a couple of minutes, relishing the moment, staring at his right hand solely holding the heavenly sword. He then slipped into the shadows of a far dark corner of the room, waiting for Andiril.

Andiril was continuing his trek toward the tower when he heard some footsteps to his right. Andiril stopped and got his javelin ready and made sure he had his two daggers and two throwing knives. He was looking to his right when he noticed a figure making its way toward him. As it was getting dark, Andiril found it hard to make out what it was. It stood up right and had rippling muscles all throughout its body, gigantic and bulging with strength. It was a beast that had been summoned during the battle of the priestesses, a beast of the earth made for destruction. Standing about eight feet tall and dark brown in color, this beast was pure muscle. No weapons did it wield, only naturally long and strong claws. Its eyes glowed a ghostly light blue. As it quickly lessened the distance between Andiril and itself, Andiril hurled his javelin at the beast, and it became lodged in the beast's throat. It fell gurgling, choking on its own blood. Andiril casually walked over to where the beast was lying and pulled the javelin out of its throat. Andiril cleaned it off, thinking to himself how easy that seemed. Just as he finished the thought, he noticed he was surrounded by about twenty more of the beasts.

He quickly leaped to his feet and got into a defensive stance. Three came at him from the back. He hurled his javelin at the one farthest left. The javelin ended up piercing the beast's heart, and it let out a screech in death. Andiril then took out two daggers from the back of his belt and lunged himself at the others, stabbing one of the two other beasts in the neck and slitting the neck of the other, both collapsing to the ground. Just as Andiril got a hold of his javelin, six more ran at him, three from either side. Once again he hurled his javelin at one of the beasts. This time it landed in the beast's left shoulder. He then took his daggers and landed a kidney shot on one of the five, sliced the stomach open of another, and stabbed through the shoulder of a third. The last two managed to knock Andiril off his feet. Then all the others jumped on top as well. There was much scratching and gnashing of teeth in the chaos that ensued. Andiril managed to make a bloody mess of the first initial beast on him, which distracted the rest of the beasts as they started to feast upon their fallen comrade. Andiril somehow escaped the beastly pile and backed away from it. He threw his javelin and struck one of the beasts in the spinal column, which caused it to let out an ear-piercing shriek. The other monsters looked and noticed their comrade on the ground dying with a javelin in his back. They then looked up and, bewildered, saw Andiril getting ready his daggers. Again, they charged at Andiril, all eleven of them. He quickly threw his two daggers, both landing embedded in the foreheads of two of the beasts. He then took his two throwing knives and ran toward the nine remaining beasts. There was one beast on either side of Andiril when he took the two knives and slit the throats of the beasts. He then threw the knives, one of them landing in the neck of one beasts and between the eyes of another. Andiril got his spear strapped on his back and plunged it into the belly of a charging beast. He quickly grabbed his javelin and threw it, and it lodged into a beast's left clavicle. With only two left, Andiril resorted to bare hand fighting. The two remaining beasts charged, and Andiril got behind one of them and broke its neck. The last one reached out toward Andiril, and Andiril broke its wrist. It backed up a bit, then Andiril charged and knocked it to the ground. Andiril proceeded to choke it till it gasped its last breath. After his job was done, Andiril retrieved and cleaned his weapons and then casually continued his hike. Not a scratch was found on his body, and he did not appear winded.

It was nightfall before Andiril walked into the tower. He paid no attention looking in all the other rooms. He knew what he wanted and where it was. Andiril just kept walking past every room on every floor till he got to the top of the tower. He walked to the end of the hall and entered the second to last room.

CHAPTER 5

ndiril opened the door and saw the ring. At last! He quickly ran over to the altar it was resting on and put it on his finger with no delay. Just as he was admiring the ring, how it looked and felt on his finger, he noticed Gūrond walking into the light from the shadows. Andiril also noticed that Gūrond had found the other gauntlet, as he was wearing it on his left hand, and the two gauntlets were glowing.

"Well, we finally meet for battle. I have been dreaming of this day and have foreseen it ever since I first took power in the East. I relish the thought of the sword of heaven slicing you in half," sneered Gūrond. Just as he said this, Gūrond pulled a massive sword out that was sheathed on his back, glowing with a greenish hue. The sword was six feet long! Only a foot shorter than Andiril's own spear! Then as Andiril pulled out his spear, Gūrond lunged at him, only to have Andiril slip out of the way. Andiril thrust his spear at Gūrond only to have the tip cut off by Gūrond's sword. Andiril backed away, stunned at the sight of his trusty spear appearing useless.

"You cannot win, Andiril. I have both gauntlets and can wield this most powerful sword. The greatest sword the land has ever seen, made in the forge of heaven by the Unknown himself," stated Gūrond, obviously proud of his new power and weapon.

Andiril remembered what he had read in the Netherworld: "In the Emerald Sword is the perfect man." Could this be right? Was it referring to Gūrond? The sword Gūrond held certainly looked to be emerald. No, impossible Andiril thought. Just then, Andiril realized his spear had been cut on an angle, a perfect javelin. The second after realizing this, Andiril hurled his spear turned javelin toward Gūrond. Gūrond got ready his sword, in a perfect stance in defense against the projectile. As the spear reached Gūrond, he cut it perfectly down the middle, from front to back. The two halves fell harmlessly to the ground on either side of Gūrond.

"I warned you. Now you must die, and my victory will be complete," stated Gūrond with a huge grin on his face.

As Gūrond lunged at Andiril, Andiril slipped to the side and grabbed Gūrond's right arm. A struggle ensued for Gūrond's sword, the sword swaying above their heads. Both Immortals took swings at each other when the opportunity arose. Occasionally a fist would meet its mark. Gūrond then knocked Andiril on the forehead with the handle of the sword. Andiril fell to the ground, his forehead bleeding. Gūrond could do nothing but stare at his brother lying there on the ground and watch Andiril bleed. No one had ever seen an Immortal bleed before. After a couple of minutes, Andiril stood up. He looked Gūrond straight in the eyes but said nothing. Gūrond got ready his sword to cause the fatal blow. He lifted his sword up above his right shoulder and brought it down diagonally across Andiril's chest, cutting it open. Andiril looked down at his blood-covered hands in disillusionment. He looked up at Gūrond in disbelief. Andiril then fell forward into a puddle of his own blood. This time Andiril did not get up after a couple of minutes of Gūrond pondering his apparent victory. After sheathing his sword, Gūrond then left the tower on the mountains and began his return to his army surrounding Andiril's fortress. Andiril just lay there on the cold floor of the tower. He managed to turn over so he was lying on his back. As he felt death taking its hold on him, the ring on his finger started to burn. Andiril was suddenly transported to another realm.

Andiril found himself where Gūrond had been. Andiril was lying in a field of the purest green grass he had ever laid eyes on. As he got up, he noticed the slice across his chest was no more nor the wound on his forehead. Andiril now noticed a huge never-ending wall in front of him with a massive gate. Andiril walked through the gate and noticed the street he was walking on was made of gems and precious stones. The main street he followed till he got to the citadel of the fortress of heaven. Andiril entered and found himself in the main hall of the citadel. He approached what appeared to be the throne. Andiril stopped. A blinding light shone forth. It was bright but did not hurt his eyes. It was piercing but had a calm, comforting feeling about it. The light lured Andiril to come forward toward the throne. As he got closer, he realized where he was and cried out, "Oh, King of Heaven, I am not worthy!" and fell to his knees.

The One on the throne said, "Arise, Servant of the Light, and look about you."

Andiril looked around and saw something that brought tears to his eyes. All his fallen comrades were standing around the edges of the throne room. Andiril fell to his knees yet again with tears of joy running down his cheeks. He then got up and ran to one of the edges of the room and started embracing all his servants, one by one. Andiril then approached the throne and asked, "How is this possible, my lord?"

"All men who fight gallantly for the light are admitted into my presence," responded the Unknown.

"Please don't think I am in any way ungrateful, but I thought all the Second Created were destined to the Netherworld," pondered Andiril.

"And you are correct except I cannot overlook anyone who fights and dies for my cause. After their physical death, I bring them here, to spend eternity with me. And now to you, Andiril, take this Emerald Sword. It will slice through bone and marrow, soul and spirit. You can wield it with the strength imbued by the ring on your finger. With it, you will cut down the Eastern Imperial Army including Gūrond. The sword I gave to Gūrond is powerful, but only a physical weapon. This Emerald Sword is ethereal and indestructible. I spoke it into existence. I did not forge it. The Emerald Sword paired with the ring you wear will enable you to rule for as long as you desire. You will not be limited to five hundred years. Now go, my servant, and cleanse the land of all evil," commanded the Unknown. It was this Emerald Sword the Netherworld inscription was referring to and thus referring to Andiril as the "perfect man." All the opposition to Gūrond, treating the Second Created the right way, being the "good guy" actually paid off! Andiril was flattered and, with all gratefulness, accepted the Emerald Sword.

When the Unknown said this, all the fearless men let out a cheer and rushed to the heavenly stables. Andiril followed more out of curiosity than anything. All the men climbed onto a horse with every horse being a different shade or color. The one horse left was different from all the rest, however. Andiril's horse was pure white. Without saying a word, Andiril sat upon his steed with all confidence. He unsheathed the Emerald Sword from his left side. He then rode out of the heavenly stable with all his men not far behind all on their steeds as well. As soon as they rode out of the stable, they started the long ride from above the clouds down to the earth.

The situation around Andiril's fortress was dire. The walls were taken, and the gate was destroyed. All the areas inside the walls were taken except for the inner citadel. The remainder of the garrison had barricaded themselves in the citadel. Gūrond had recently rejoined his army on the field, and just as he was walking up to his general Galdier, a great resounding trumpet blasted out from the heavens. At that, Gūrond, Galdier, and the whole of the Imperial Army turned to see the clouds in the sky roll back as a scroll and a piercing light shone down. Then, something unthinkable was seen—horsemen suddenly came down from the clouds. The horsemen rode down from the clouds in the sky toward the earth below. The horses got ever closer to the ground, but they didn't touch the ground; they sort of glided about a foot from it and galloped toward the army of the East. As the heavenly host of horsemen got closer to the army of the East, they spread out so as to engulf Gūrond's entire army upon meeting it. Gūrond got ready his sword, as he knew of nothing else he could do, and just stood there expressionless, waiting for his imminent death. The horde of heavenly horsemen came ever closer, the horses huffing and the men yelling out a great shout.

As all this was happening, Gūrond saw a disturbing sight; Andiril was leading these heavenly horsemen! Suddenly a fear of judgment came over him, and an unmistakable expression of fear came to his face. As Andiril sliced through Gūrond's chest, armor and all, the expression of fear left Gūrond's face as he collapsed into a puddle of his own blood and died there. Galdier was the next to be killed, his head being chopped off and flung from his body. This was the fate of the entire Imperial Army. The horsemen spread out along the entire front of the army and just went forward, annihilating everybody as they went. Bodies lay dead where they were standing just seconds ago. The horsemen then entered through the breached gate, and the fate of the Imperial Army inside the fortress was the same as those outside: death. Soon the land was cleared of the Imperial filth.

Andiril rode up to his citadel and got off his horse. He walked in toward his throne room. As he entered the room, he noticed the inhabitants of the fortress in the throne room; and as soon as Andiril started toward his throne chair, a voice from heaven announced, "This is my servant Andiril whom you shall worship and obey without question. Any who oppose him shall be immediately judged by me, the Unknown, and cast into the Netherworld."

All the Second Created bowed before Andiril. He was now the undisputed ruler of all the land between the West and East citadels. The land was free from tyranny, and peace now reigned. Hereby was how the Kingdom of Andiril was established and endured for ten thousand years hereafter.

www.ingramcontent.com/pod-product-compliance
Lightning Source LLC
Chambersburg PA
CBHW041025170626

46815CB00001B/9